P9-CRA-685

For Honey Boy, and in loving memory of Mary and Antonio DiCarlo.

I wish to thank Rebecca Stevens, my editor, for her guidance.

Grazie, Alessia Giovannini.

—R.M.G.

To the often unforeseen rewards of cooperative efforts.
—J.L.G.

Andiamo, Weasel!

By Rose Marie Grant

Illustrated by Jon Goodell

Alfred A. Knopf • New York

Once, on the golden fields of Tuscany, there lived a weasel and a crow. . . .

"*Buongiorno,* my friend!" said the weasel one spring day.
"Nice weather for planting corn."

"*Sì,*" said the crow. "You're right, weasel."

"This is such a *grande* job for such a *piccola* crow," the weasel
continued. "But if I help—*presto!*—the job will be done, and when
harvest comes we can split the crop. Okay?"

"*Va bene,* weasel!" agreed the crow.

Side by side, they sang as they sowed:
"Tra la la la la! *Funiculì, funiculà!*"

Weeks passed, and the field
needed weeding. . . .

"*Andiamo,* weasel! Let's go! It's time to tend the corn!" called the crow.

"Crow, didn't you know?" moaned the weasel. "I fell into a hole; my leg is broken."

"What a shame!" lamented the crow. "It is such a *grande* job and I am so *piccola*!"

"I'm sorry, crow, but if you do this now, I promise to help with the next job," the weasel vowed.

"*Va bene,* weasel!" agreed the crow.

Feeling sorry for the weasel, the little crow flew off to work the crop.

"*Mamma mia!* What a poor weasel!" sighed the crow.

Months passed, and the corn grew tall and golden. . . .

"*Andiamo*, weasel! It's harvest time!" called the crow.

"*Via!* I'm in such pain." The weasel quickly hid in his bed. "First my leg caused me to limp. Now my back is suffering. I'm sorry, crow, but if you do this now, I promise to help with the next job."

"*Mamma mia!* What a lying weasel!" scoffed the crow. "What am I to do? It is such a *grande* job and I am so *piccola*!"

But off she went to cut the corn.

When the last of the crop was stacked in piles, storm clouds rolled across the sky. The crow flew quickly to get the weasel.

"*Per favore!*" begged the crow. "Please help me get the corn into the barn. Rain is coming and the crop will be lost! *Andiamo,* weasel!"

The weasel snored, pretending to be asleep.

"*Mamma mia!* What a weaselly weasel!" groaned the crow. "What am I to do? It is such a *grande* job and I am so *piccola!*"

But with one wheelbarrow, the little crow worked all night.
When the final load was safe, she fell fast asleep to the sound of
pelting rain on the roof.

"Chicchirichì!" cried the rooster. The little crow awoke with a start to find the corn—every last ear—gone. Only the husks remained.

In shock, she flew to see the weasel.

"My corn! It's gone!" cried the crow.

"Sì." The weasel pointed to the neatly stacked golden ears. "I promised that I would do the next job. So, *piccola* crow, I divided our crop," laughed the weasel. "And you get the husks!" The weasel slammed the door.

"*Mamma mia!* What a rotten weasel! What am I to do? I am so *piccola*!"

But the little crow got angrier and angrier as she thought about her stolen corn.

"*Vendetta!*" cried the crow as she whirled overhead. "Revenge! Where is that wolf?"

She had not flown far when she spotted him.

"*Aiuto! Aiuto!* Help! Help!" begged the crow.

"*Che cosa?*" snapped the wolf. "What's the matter?"

The crow told her sad story.

"So what do you want of me?" snarled the wolf.

"Just what you're doing now. Snap . . . snarl . . . look big. The weasel will run away and then I can reclaim my corn."

"What's in it for me?" demanded the wolf.

"*Polenta* for the winter? Maybe *lire*? I can sell some of the crop," the crow offered.

"My stomach does not growl for corn or money," the wolf answered. "But if I could eat my fill of pizza, and if you could make me laugh as I have never laughed before . . . maybe I would help you."

"*Va bene!*" agreed the crow. "First you will eat. *Andiamo,* wolf! Let's go to the *signora*'s house. She is making tasty pizza!"

When they got to the garden of the *signora,* the crow swooped and pecked at her tomatoes. As the *signora* chased her with a broom, the crow called out, "*Buon appetito!* Enjoy your meal!" and the wolf hungrily stuffed himself with the saucy pies.

"*Brava!*" cried the wolf. "*Grazie!* Thank you!"

"*Prego!*" said the crow. "You're welcome! *Andiamo,* wolf! Now you will laugh."

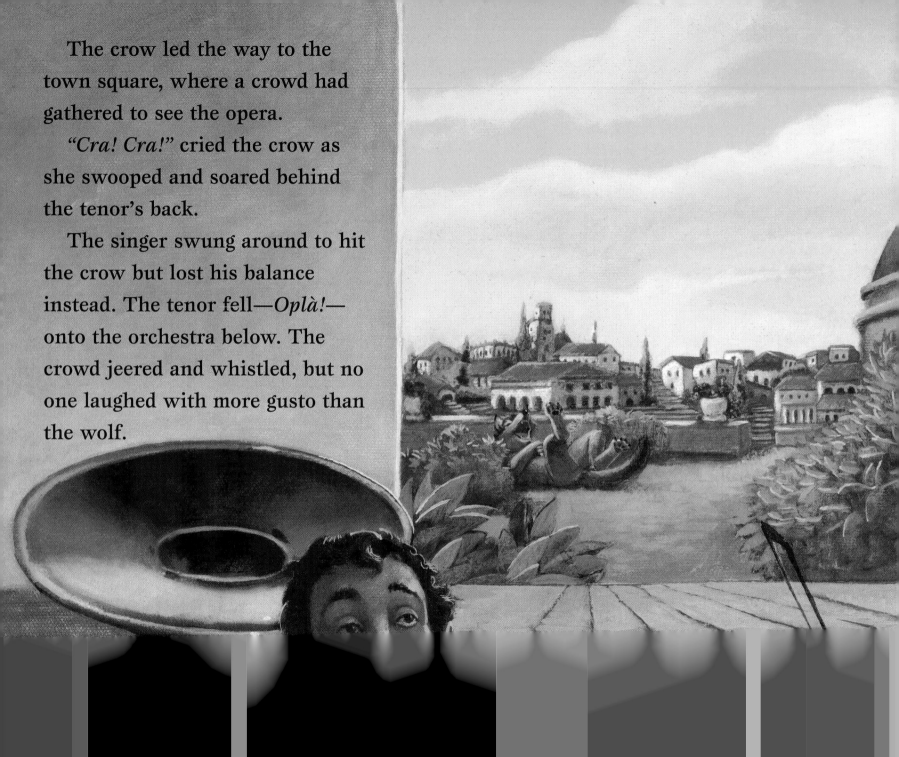

The crow led the way to the town square, where a crowd had gathered to see the opera.

"*Cra! Cra!*" cried the crow as she swooped and soared behind the tenor's back.

The singer swung around to hit the crow but lost his balance instead. The tenor fell—*Oplà!*—onto the orchestra below. The crowd jeered and whistled, but no one laughed with more gusto than the wolf.

"*Brava!*" The wolf smoothed the crow's ruffled feathers with his
sandpaper tongue. "*Grazie!*" chuckled the wolf.

"*Prego!*" said the crow. "*Andiamo,* wolf! It is time to see the
weasel."

When they arrived, the weasel was sitting down to a dinner of *polenta.*

"Go hide," ordered the crow, "and I'll tell you when to come out."

"*Va bene,*" agreed the wolf, hiding from view.

"*Andiamo,* weasel! Open up!" called the crow.

"*Delizioso!*" mocked the weasel, opening the door. "Our corn is the finest in the countryside. Yum!" The weasel kissed the tip of his paw.

"*Disgraziato!*" shouted the crow. "You wretch!" She flew at the weasel in a rage, forgetting the wolf. The fierce little crow pecked at him with such force that the weasel squealed with fright, "*Aiuto! Aiuto!* Help! Help!"

"What a cowardly weasel!" the crow cried as he bolted down the road.

"*Arrivederci! Ciao! Addio!*" she shouted, waving good-bye with her little wings. "And good riddance!"

"*Brava! Brava!*" cheered the wolf. "What a performance! *Fantastica!*"

"No thanks to you," snapped the crow.

"But you didn't need me, my friend," answered the wolf. "You may be *piccola* in size, but you are *grande* in spirit: You grew the corn; you tricked the *signora*; you chased the weasel. And best of all, you are a very funny little crow!"

"*Grazie!* Now do you think we could laugh our way into the barn with this corn?" teased the crow.

"*Sì*, and then maybe later— more pizza?" asked the wolf.

"*Va bene!*" agreed the crow. "*Andiamo,* my friend!"

Side by side, the soprano crow and
the baritone wolf sang as they worked:
"Tra la la la la! *Funiculì, funiculà!*"

Glossary

addio (ah-*dee*-oh) farewell

aiuto! (ah-*yoo*-toh) help!

andiamo! (ahnd-*yah*-moh) let's go!

arrivederci (ah-ree-veh-*dehr*-chee) good-bye

brava! (*brah*-vah) good for you!

buon appetito (bwohn ahp-peh-*tee*-toh) good appetite

buongiorno! (bwohn-*johr*-noh) good morning!

che cosa? (kay *koh*-sah) what's the matter?

chicchirichì! (kee-kee-ree-*kee*) cock-a-doodle-doo!

ciao (chow) so long

delizioso (deh-leets-*yoh*-soh) delicious

disgraziato (*dees*-grah-tsee-*ah*-toh) wretch

fantastica (fan-*tah*-stee-kah) fantastic

grande (*grahn*-day) big

grazie (*grahts*-yay) thank you

lire (*lee*-ray) Italian currency

mamma mia! (*mahm*-mah *mee*-yah) good gracious!

per favore (pair fah-*voh*-ray) please

piccola (*peek*-koh-lah) small

polenta (poh-*lehn*-tah) cornmeal mush

prego! (*preh*-goh) you're welcome!

presto! (*pres*-toh) quickly!

sì (see) yes

signora (seen-*yoh*-rah) Mrs. or Madam

va bene (vah *beh*-nay) all right

via! (*vee*-yah) go away!

THIS IS A BORZOI BOOK PUBLISHED BY ALFRED A. KNOPF

Text copyright © 2002 by Rose Marie Grant ☼ Illustrations copyright © 2002 by Jon Goodell

All rights reserved under International and Pan-American Copyright Conventions. Published in the United States of America by Alfred A. Knopf, a division of Random House, Inc., New York, and simultaneously in Canada by Random House of Canada Limited, Toronto. Distributed by Random House, Inc., New York.

KNOPF, BORZOI BOOKS, and the colophon are registered trademarks of Random House, Inc.

www.randomhouse.com/kids

Library of Congress Cataloging-in-Publication Data
Grant, Rose Marie.
Andiamo, weasel! / by Rose Marie Grant ; illustrated by Jon Goodell.
p. cm.
ISBN 0-375-80607-5 (trade) — ISBN 0-375-90607-X (lib. bdg.)
[1. After a crow is tricked by a lazy weasel, she finds that she can deal with him all by herself even though she is very small. Includes a glossary of Italian words used.
2. Crows—Fiction. 3. Weasels—Fiction. 4. Wolves—Fiction. 5. Self-reliance—Fiction.] I. Goodell, Jon, ill. II. Title.
PZ7.G7685 An 2002
[E]—dc21 2001037726

Printed in the United States of America
August 2002

10 9 8 7 6 5 4 3 2 1
First Edition